How Billy Hippo learned to swim

KT-116-602

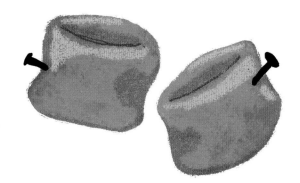

Vivian French

Hannah Foley

This book
belongs
to

_ _ _ _ _ _ _ _ _ _ _ _ _ _ _

For Tess, to read to her little brothers. – VF

For Viv and Jessica, because of love and cake. – HF

Thanks to Viv and Hannah for taking the plunge with us.
Special thanks once again to Dave Gray and Paul Croan. - LDB

Published by Little Door Books 2018
This edition published 2018

ISBN: 978-0-9927520-8-8

Text copyright © Vivian French 2018
Illustrations copyright © Hannah Foley 2018

The right of Vivian French and Hannah Foley to be identified as author and
illustrator of this work has been asserted in accordance with the Copyright,
Designs and Patents Act 1988.
All rights reserved. No part of this publication may be reproduced, stored in
a retrieval system, or transmitted in any form or by any means, electronic, mechanical,
photocopying, recording or otherwise, without prior permission of the publishers.

A CIP catalogue record for this book is available from the British Library.

Little Door Books

Email: mail@littledoorbooks.co.uk
Web: www.littledoorbooks.co.uk
Twitter: @littledoorbooks

Little Billy Hippo was standing on the river bank.

"I don't like swimming," he said. "The water's too cold and wet."

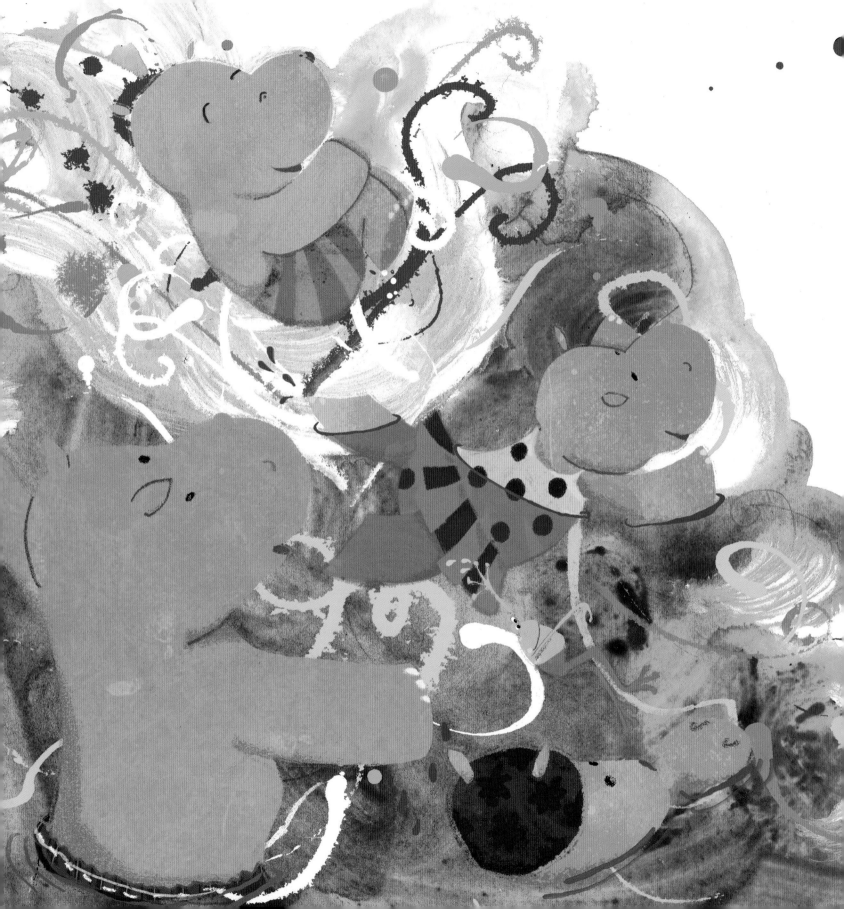

"Nonsense, Billy," said his dad.
"All hippos LOVE swimming!"

"That's right," said his mum. "Look at us."

"Come on, Billy," said his brother Ben.
"Just jump in."

"No!" said Billy. "It's too cold."

"Water is LOVELY!" said his sister Betty.
"You can swim and swirl and wallow in water."

Billy shook his head. "It's too wet."

"Why don't I give you a piggy back?" said his dad.

"That's too scary," said Billy.

"Come and swim with me," said his mum,
and she climbed out of the river.

"NO!" said Billy, and he backed away.

"I'll show you how," said Ben, and he dived into the river with a SPLASH!

"OOOOH," said Billy. "That made me cold!"

"Watch me wallow," said Betty, and she jumped into the river with an even bigger SPLASH!

"OOOOH!" said Billy. "That made me wet!"

His mum laughed. "I'm coming to get you."

"Me, too," said his dad.

"NO!" said Billy, and he went backwards as fast as he could...

and he tripped...

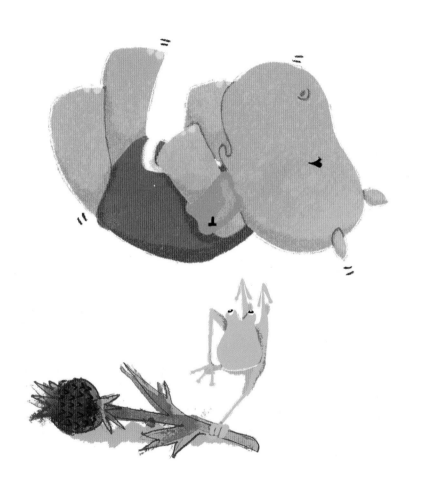

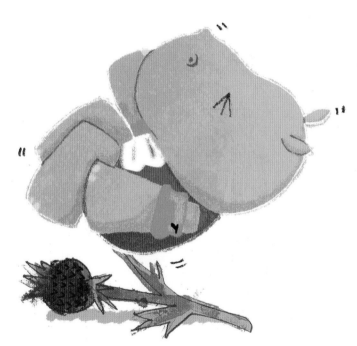

and he sat on a thistle.

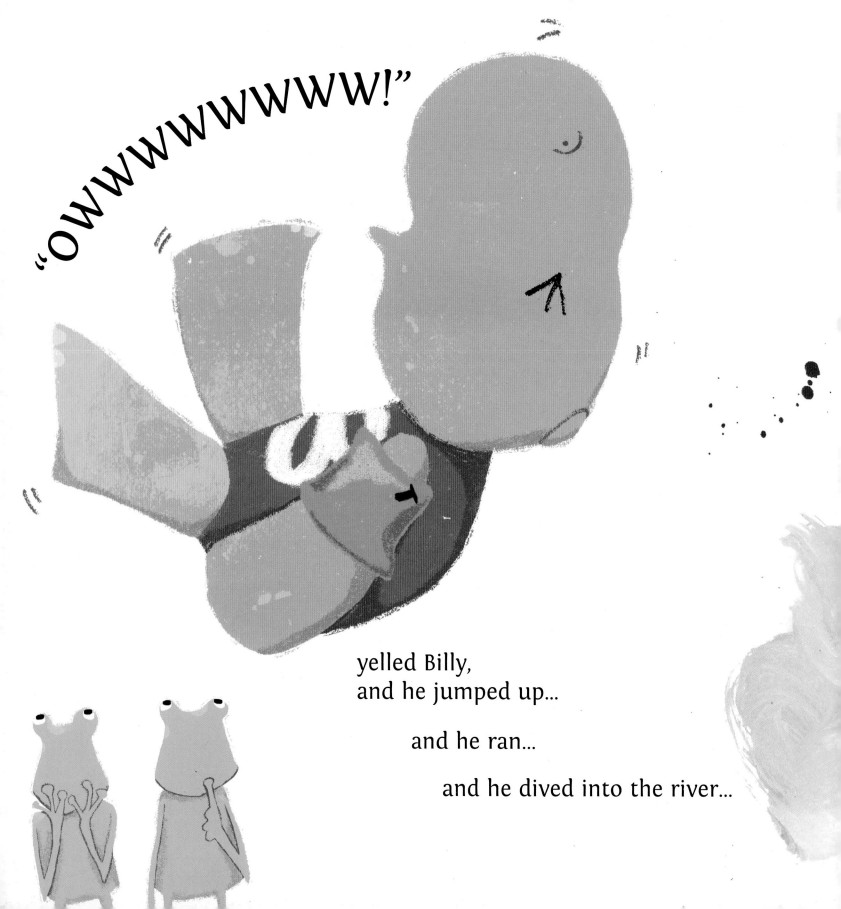

"OWWWWWWWW!"

yelled Billy,
and he jumped up...

and he ran...

and he dived into the river...

with the biggest splash of all.

"Well done, Billy!" said his mum.

"Good work, Billy!" said his dad.

"Hurrah!" said Ben and Betty.

"GLUG GLUG GLUG,"

said Billy as he sank to the bottom of the river.

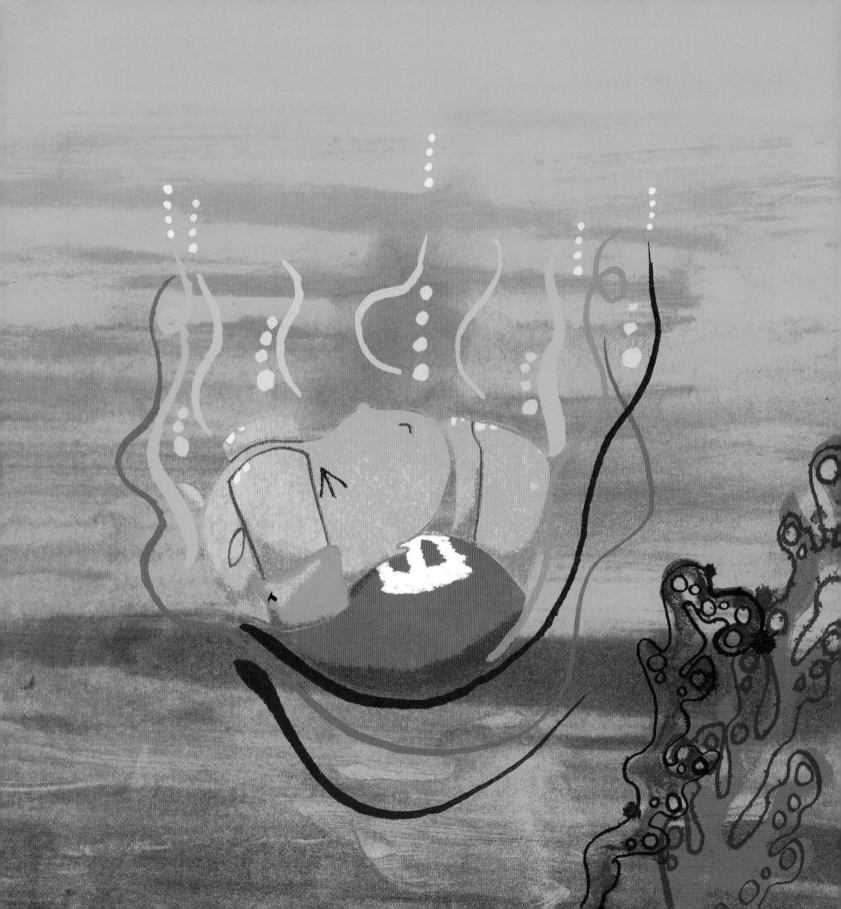

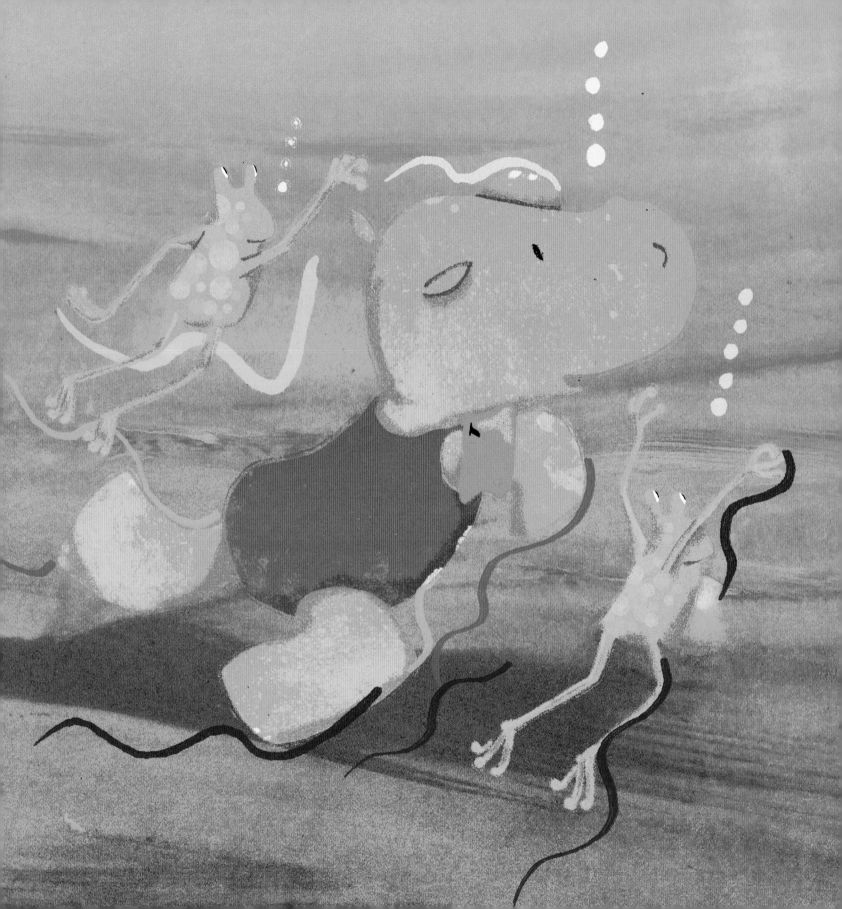

GLUG,"

GLUG

"GLUG

as he swirled and he wallowed...